WRAPPED UP FEELINGS

-Nandini Shrivasatava

FanatiXx Publication

AM/56, Basanti Colony, Rourkela 769012, Odisha
ISO 9001:2015 CERTIFIED
Website: *www.fanatixx.in*

"WRAPPED UP FEELINGS"

By: Nandini Shrivastava

ISBN: 978-93-89557-72-5

English Poetry & Quotes

1st Edition

Book Formatting: MAYURI VALANJ
Book Cover: SAGAR SAMAL
Presented By: REASONS AND LAUGHTER

<u>DISCLAIMER</u>

<u>This is a work of fiction. Our editors have tried their best to edit the content of all the author/authors and check the plagiarism. All the write-ups in this book are unique and are only published in this book.</u>

<u>In case any plagiarism or error is found, the author is the sole responsible and not the publisher.</u>

Acknowledgement

The completion of this anthology would not have been possible without the incredible rate of work of our talented team as well as co-authors. Immense thanks to entire core team who gave their precious time for this book.

A ton of thanks to our publication team Reasons and Laughter without you this would not have been possible.

I would like to thank every co-author for trusting me and for making my dream come true.

Contents

AUTHOR'S DESK

Nandini Shrivastava Daughter of Mr. Sanjay Shrivastava and Mrs. Shikha Shrivastava was brought up in Jabalpur, Madhya Pradesh.

Currently, she is pursuing her 12th from commerce stream. seen her interest stoop towards novels and literature, she get herself towards chasing her passion for writing. She is a co-author in many anthologies.

Contact her through Email (nandinishri33@gmail.com)

FOUNDER

JAPNEET KAUR

Japneet Kaur, daughter of Mr. Surjeet Singh and Mrs. Dilpreet Kaur was brought up in Indirapuram, UP. She is pursuing German language and BA programming course from Delhi University. She is a passionate writer who loves to pen down her emotions and environment and strive to make her parents proud. She is even working on her very first novel making her one step closer to her goal.

Instgram : @sheedreamss

EDITOR

MAYURI VALANJU

Mayuri Valanju, resident of Mumbai. She is a commerce graduate pursuing higher education. Social Media Head of Fanatixx and Fanatixx Publications. Co-author of many anthologies. Her debut book is 'Spectrum of Thoughts'. Writing is Peace for her. She is addict of Korean, Turkish and Chinese dramas. Coffee is her love and sound of book pages flipping like her the most. Connecting with people and talking to them is what she loves.

You can find her on instagram @scribblers_abode.

DESIGNER

SAGAR SAMAL

Sagar Samal is a Photographer, Image Manipulation
and Colour Grading Artist.
Hardworking with a "Create Something Awesome"
Mentality.
A graduate in Bachelor of Computer Application but an
Artist By Heart.

Instagram : photosign.cf

OPEN
LETTERS

To Doraemon,

This is neither a love letter not a heartbreak one. This is
not meant for any lover but for someone who is my best
friend and always loved me like no one ever did. He is the
one who gave me a reason to live and never gave up on
me. This is for the one who loved me selflessly and
unconditionally even when everyone left me I still had
him. Yes this is for you Doraemon. This is to pay you
gratitude to whatever you did for me. I was always an
absent minded guy with a lot of problems in my life. I've
never done well in any aspects of life. Though I've tried a
lot to be someone people would admire but I always
failed in getting what I deserve. May it be studies or
friendship or love or anything, I failed in all but you
never let me fail in your friendship. You were always
there with me in my ups and downs and never let me fall.
Due to my problems I was in depression and no one
wanted to talk to me because they use to think that I m
fool and that I don't deserve to be loved, but you loved
me and proved the world that I deserve to be loved. You
are my biggest asset. I love you so much. Though I never
say it and I nag a lot in front of you and even fight with
you but no one can ever understand me the way you did
and no one can love me the way you do. Without
Doraemon there is no Nobita. You r my lifeline and I hope
everyone should have a Doraemon in their life. Especially
those who give their 100% to everything and everyone
still end up getting hurt. I wish the boy who is getting
bullied everyday had you, the healthy girl out there
whom people body shame had you, the students with low
great but high dreams had you, the kindest heartbroken
girl who every night cries to sleep had you, the boy who
got ditched by his love had you, the orphans who crave
for family had you, the widow who lost the reason to live

had you, the girl in depression had you. I wish, the good hearted people who are suffering and crying every night to sleep still getting up with the fake smile which looks like real had you.

Life would be so easy if people had a friend like you who was always there with them no matter what. Who was selfless? At least it would have given them a reason to live like I had after I got you

From yours and only yours,
Nobita.

Japneet Kaur ~

To my parents ,

At this point in my life, I'm considered an adult. Yes, maybe sometimes I don't completely act like it, but that's part of life, right? As I'm growing up, I realize just how much you did for me. And, for that, I need to truly thank you – something I don't think I've appropriately done to date. Dad, thank you for telling me what I'm capable of. For giving me the support that I needed to build a dream to chase after. Mom, thank you for making me realize that I'm worth everything in this world. That I must be treated like a queen, and that I should never settle for less than what I deserve. I know i have troubled you many Times. I hurt you many Times. But then also you forgive me for my each and every mistake. This make me realize your unconditional love. To both of you, Mom and Dad, thank you for showing me true love in its rarest form, what it feels like, and how it can extend beyond life's obstacles and challenges. Without each of you, I'd be nowhere near the person.

Yours daughter,

Nandini Shrivastava ~

To my person,

I think that you are placed into peoples lives for a reason. Sometimes I wonder how I got so lucky and what I have done to deserve a friend like you. People have come and gone out of my life, but for some reason you never left. Your friendship is one of the greatest gifts I have ever received.

I cannot give any Name to this relationship. But i must say that i really blessed to have u in my life. U always make me feel better and try to divert my mind whenever i feel low, depressed, and frustrated.

I could write a book about the positive affect you have had on my life. Your heart is of the purest that I have ever known. The love and compassion that you show for others is special. I am really blessed.

You believed in me when I didn't believe in myself. You loved me when I was hard to love. You listened to me when I didn't have a voice. But most importantly, you never gave up on me. That is special. Thankyou so much for always being There for me.Thank you for deciding to join me on this crazy journey we call life. And most importantly thank you so much for allowing me to be a part of your life.

Yours,

Someone

To the person I love,

You have given me a reason for smiling once again. You have filled my life with peaceful dreams and you have shared your heartfelt secrets, and your trust that you have given me, you showed me how to fall again to laugh, love and see.

I love you because you made me smile when I almost forgotten how to. I love you because you have a huge and honest heart. I love you because you actually put efforts into me. I love you because nobody has ever given me the love that you have given me and you are the one that could ever love me this way. I LOVE YOU BECAUSE YOU ALWAYS MAKE ME FEEL THAT I AM WORTH SOMETHING. I love You because you are simply you.

Yours

Bhawana Ketarppal

To My Parents,

The precious gift which we received from God throughout our life is our parents who gave us birth and made us worthy for glancing this beautiful world. Nothing is much worthy than there blessings and support in every part of life. They are the epitome of selfless love. The sacrifices they made were countless. The happiness they gave was eternal. Being with them is the heavenly part of this world. Nothing is more comparable than there presence in our life. Accepting our imperfection with all the perfect reasons is just done by our parents. Irreplaceable soul of this world is our parents. Something we can do is to make them proud with our deeds.

Yours Daughter,

Pratikshya Parhi

Letter To The GOD

Here I am with all the bruises and burns, with a cold blooded heart refusing to pump further, Blood dripping through the cuts of my fingers. The unforgivable pain in my lower abdomen departing my soul slowly through the inquisitive eyes of mine. Is it all a curse to my gender? Still how many more!! Now why me?

-Aarthi Selvam

Appreciation of mighty

You may be simple in your sight

 what you utter may be right

your goldens took me to the groove

 Confidence of your's helped me prove

 without it smile may be casuality

 at the instant death of live may be probability

 The first to last and the last to vision

 Darling of mine saved me from fission

You are a angel with a sword

Appreciation of yours doesn't pose a word

 came in my life as a star

 not a pole but a par light in day and darkness at night

 be mine forever and never leave my side

~ Aryan Verma

<u>MIRROR</u>

The day still haunts me; 21st June,

The sky was giggling with sun rays,

And the humidity was not turbulent,

The comforting monsoon has arrived,

But I could not escape the scathing heat of my past,

It scratched my skin and made me bleed,

Extreme pain blurred my vision,

And those utterances numbed my senses for a decade-

" Please forget me. I am not able to continue this anymore"

Your cries and laugh simultaneously could not melt my stony heart.

I was adamant in my declaration.

I knew if I can play this part well: You will be happy forever.

And what more my beloved, a living dead body who is ardently in love with you can ask for.

~ Tritrishna ghosh

FEELINGS

Low and high,

Mixed feelings every time,

Are not permanent,

Change every time,

Depend upon the atmosphere,

Though it's very true,

For better results

Never be so obsessed with Feelings.....

-Shipra khanna

<u>Live and endure</u>

Keeping you inside, Throwing everyone aside.

Not letting anyone to enter, Negative feel you nurture.

Let go the pain, Else there's no gain.

Don't hurt yourself, Write and safeguard in a bookshelf.

Enduring or crying doesn't work, Venting out or letting go gives a perk.

Leaving the piece, Gives you peace.

Being positive, Gets rid of negative(s).

Laugh, love, live,
Have a nature to forgive.

Gone are the days, you sit and worry,
Many responsibilities you have to carry.

Happy is the child in heart, Maintaining it safe is an art.

Don't stress your mind, Be a little kind.

Have a happy soul, Let life play it's role.

-Phalgunii Jagadeesh

<u>*LET ME FLY*</u>

Dear brother,

I know you love me,

I love you too.

You became my bodyguard,

When our father beat me.

You became my teacher,

When I was weak in maths.

You became my healer,

When my heart was broken.

You even became my ATM card,

When I lost mine.

Dear brother,

I know you love me,

I love you too .

You Were Always There ,

Whenever I needed You.

But Trust Me,

This Time let me do it

I can do it.

I know it's going to be hard outside

Since I may not have

A perfect bodyguard,

A freaking teacher

Or a best healer...

But trust me,

This Time let me do it,

I can do it.

Let me fly.

~ Vishnu E

<u>One in the morning</u>

It was one in the morning,

And I was in your arms,

And you were in my heart,

And our words were minimal,

And our love was not,

And silence was all around us,

And, for a little while, within us too.

It is one in the morning,

And I'm on the bathroom floor,

And you're in my thoughts,

And my words are minimal,

And my grief is Not,

And silence is all around me,

Except, within me.

-MIRA A HENSS

Days longing

Days passed,

But our friendship did not passed.

 Moments gone,

But our Memories did not.

When i was great,

You were there,

When I was Bad,

You were there too.

Whatever it maybe,

Wherever it maybe,

I know We will all be the same,

Because some relationships are made to be

eternal.

We Laughed, we lied,

We fought,we cried.

To keep each one of us happy, We always

tried.

Life's 2nd Greatest gift are You itself for me,

After all i only got you now With me.

Chaithanya

<u>*BEAUTY*</u>

She was a loser, as everyone says..

Because she didn't have that

perfectly tuned face

or a well maintained figure,

but inside those ugly features

beats a heart which tried to love

everyone unconditionally. .

But how a world which stands on materialism,

deeply immersed in the ocean of superficiality

can ever realize the glow of beauty that

 blooms from inside...

~ Monsumi Borah

My Heart

Heart, O heart , why do you cry,

Still having this feeling,

That all must die.

For the dagger is pierced through you,

Without even a slightest clue.

And your blood have made skies red ,

Which felt like millennia ago was blue.

O heart, I know you're so broken,

But worry not;

For the world is full of adventure ,

And far more miraculous tokens.

Fly up high to touch the sky ,

Time to celebrate with a grateful joy.

For today's a gift, and tomorrow a surprise.

~ Kunal Thorat

<u>Yes!! You My Friend</u>

Someone to call upon when problems appear

Someone who lifts me up to make my problems disappear

Someone who enriches my life in a myriad of ways

Someone who envelops my heart with love, joy and prayers

Someone who helps the road seem straighter

Someone who always make me feel that I deserve much better

Yes, that someone is you my friend

You are all this and more of my friend

Together one day we will make our friendship proud

Even if we are dead our friendship will never get covered with shroud......

-Shivanshi Shrivastava

Listen my sub-conscious

Thou are a bunch of memories, joyous and bad,

Reminiscence of which at times makes me ecstatic and

at times sad.

Thou are my most intimate partner in life's meander,

Thou aid my each prudent epiphany and harbinger.

You have safely preserved my each upheaval and

decline,

Which never let's me the forget the real identity of mine.

You give me the impetus in my each endeavour,

Thou have abetted each blissful experience that today I

savour.

Thou have been manipulated a lot by every single guy of

my life,

And have the deep inscribed impressions of my each glee

and strife.

Still I urge you to stay unaffected and ignorant,

Suppress the deterring vibes and always keep me

exuberant.

-Shrajan Tiwari

<u>*Introverts!*</u>

They talk a lot.

Yes they do talk a lot.

Not with a bunch of people.

But at least with a few people.

They go for deep talk.

Instead of weather's talk.

Don't tag them as shy.

Don't take their silence as their attitude

Let them talk to the sky

Let then Savoie's some hours of solitude.

Let them have some freedom of choice.

To decide how to raise their voice.

~ Mahek Jain

<u>I'LL BE HOME SOON</u>

My son packed his bag,

Tears filled the eyes of this old hag.

"I'll be home soon," he lied,

For years I believed and my heart sighed.

My son didn't settle abroad,

The reason why he left is worth laud.

"I'll be home soon," he lied,

For years on his wrist by his sister,

No rakhi had been tied.

My son settled on borders,

He executed all the orders

"I'll be home soon," he lied,

For years lurking him his wife cried.

My son was so far,

He was fighting a war.

"I'll be home soon," he lied.

For years what connection had been tied?

My grandson who is just 5 years old,

"You are his father," he has been told.

My son wore sometimes green, brown or blue

He protected us all, me and you.

"I'll be home soon," he lied,

Years before 'he should become brave' his father always tried.

Alike his martyred father his life was full of discipline,

Both their personalities were so sheen.

My son never showed up yet

Then came the postman bringing fate.

Bringing a letter, Making us feel better.

"I'll be home soon," he still lied.

One day he finally came.

That was the day when 'martyr' was attached to his name.

The tricolour became his shroud,

Being a mother to a martyred soldier and thus a veer nari,

I was so proud

~ Wadkar Samreen Shabab

The TAJ

The pride of India

That stands on Yamuna's bank

Which in the 7 Wonders holds a rank.

In the state of Uttar Pradesh it resides

In the glorious and designated city of Agra it abides.

It stands tall revealing its pride and glory

It epitomizes their love story.

It trumpets its marble structure,dome and minarets all with intricate works

Thus, 'to visit again' every visitor lurks.

It is surrounded by lavish gardens

And the ASI diligently looks after it just like wardens.

Its reflection is worth seeing in its pool

And its shimmering marble in the moonlit is so cool.

~ Wadkar Samreen Shabab

Rays of Hope

As I sit near the window side,

Penning down my thoughts,

My feelings and my crushing emotions:

 That has dried.

My feelings overpowered by the wings,

Craving for the feelings,

Pour some emotions and some good deeds.

And then I try to whisk.

Dragging my soul to the barren land,

Where I have lost myself,

I couldn't find.

Hoping for the good times.

Deep down inside I am struggling.

Holding my hand in times of despair,

Never allowing me to fall apart,

Hoping for the times you will care.

Capturing the memories I shared,

Transforming them into my sheer strength,

Donning a new mask to face,

The worlds at its glory and pace.

Letting go of the darkness of my past,

Holding on the tender threads that last.

Hoping for the light ray that falls,

The ray of hope peeping through the dark.

-Ritika Mahto

<u>CAPTIVE</u>

I , am trying so hard to forget you.

I , just wish that you leave ,

my dreams and stop clouding my thoughts.

You can't , because you didn't

choose to stay in there.

I , imprinted you there.

I , held you captive in my mind ,

cause that was the only place,

I ,would call you mine..

~ Zainab Shaikh

Menstrual cycle

She paints this town every month red

Though badly suffering from cramp in bed.

For naturally bleeding should be shy

Why a little bloodstain on her dress makes her cry.

 She feels proud of herself,

She still does her chores on such days without

anyone's help.

Not physically but it made her mentally strong

Can a Natural process also be called wrong?

Being a woman she feels proud,

No other beings can survive by bleeding

She Can

Say it loud.

~ Sumit Saha

<u>Maybe.</u>

Maybe my life isn't as perfect as yours,

Maybe my family isn't as rich as yours,

Maybe my idea isn't as brilliant as yours,

But maybe,

I don't care about what's mine and what's yours.

Maybe my vocabulary isn't as good as yours,

Maybe my dress isn't as beautiful as yours,

Maybe my friend isn't as sweet as yours,

But maybe,

I don't care about what's mine and what's yours.

Maybe my mom isn't as lovely as yours,

 Maybe my father isn't as loving as yours,

Maybe my brother isn't as affectionate as yours,

But maybe,

I don't care about what's mine and what's yours.

 But,

Maybe my life is way more peaceful than yours,

Maybe my family is happier than yours,

Maybe my idea is better than yours,

Yes,

I definitely don't care about what's mine and what's

yours.

Maybe my vocabulary is more accurate than yours,

Maybe my dress is more lively than yours,

Maybe my friend is more realistic than yours,

Yes,

I definitely don't care about what's mine and what's

yours.

Maybe my mom is more hardworking than yours,

Maybe my father is more sacrificing than yours,

Maybe my brother is more protective than yours.

Yes,

I definitely don't care about what's mine and what's

yours.

But,

Don't you dare compare what's mine to yours,

But if you do, Dear, take care because of one day,

What's mine won't be mine,

And what's yours will not be yours.

~ Vidushi Agarwal

"The long distance Trauma"

The long distance Trauma

 Wanting him in my arms,

Is what I wish from far.

 Imagining this,

Makes my heart pound.

As the scene shuts,

Everything shatters down.

This is what happens when you are not around.

 The distance won't seperate us,

 From the inside I knew.

But waiting for you,

Made my day gloom.

 Just a thought of us together,

 Made the grey clouds move.

 At the end when we talked,

 Facing the screen,

The tears raced down like a beam.

How could you wipe them?

I wondered.

But your words,

 Made my tears surrender.

Everything turns perfect as it moves,

But a part of me still misses you.

~ Niyati Desai

<u>DEFINITION OF UNKNOWN</u>

It's beautiful how you change

 Just to forget Someone

Change your Approach

Change your number

Delete the other person's number

But your mobile still saves it as

Unknown And just like the default settings

of your mobile

You realize how definition of unknown got changed

 You read quotes of inspiration

 You feel the change and then

 you come across the quote Written by someone unknown

 And that's when you realize how defination of unknown has

changed

Some beautiful piece written by

 Someone You check out its author Source

says its unknown

And that's when you realize how defination of unknown

changed

A word Once attached to person with a definite intent It itself

gets attached to him

However unknown that person is right now

 The word unknown becomes so familiar

 The string of buried memories of him make this unknown

entity just like family

 And that's when u realize how defination of unknown changed

the sudden past premonition strikes

 And you realize how much you have always feared "the

Unknown "

~(Stashedviews) Nikita

Characterless justice

Dragged down to ground,

forced to be undressed

Nails and tooth were stabbed,

strangleholded, grips in groups with guilt

Faught pulverized war with myself,

alone with many of those evil existences

Squawked, beseeched for help,

none came out of their dead mindsets.

I am baffled being alive when I feel like dead.

I have been persecuted and vitiated while yet to be tested.

Still character less

they call me character less.

They judge me more when they helped me less.

Still character less,

still character less,

they call me still character less.

~ Bhaskar Malakar

<u>Warrior</u>

Numbness

The only emotion

I have

Lost

have no one

to save me from myself

There's no way back

Time moves forward

My demons attack

I'm not a coward

I'll make it through

I see the light

The only thing I know

is how to fight.

-RANVIR RANA

<u>Take me back to the night we met</u>

Take me back to the night we met

Where the time stopped

and flower witnessed our love,

Take me back to the night we met

Where there were only you and me

Where the air of love is flowing,

Take me back to the night we met

When we shared our first kiss

When we both got drunk in love,

Take me back to the night we met

Where the magic happened,

Take me back to the night we met

Before I forget everything

Before it becomes all blurry,

Take me back to the night we met

Where all this happened.

~ Purti Rohatgi

<u>You are never mine</u>

I am waiting for you looking at the moon

In the hope that you will come soon

You will grab my hand one day

And passionately our eyes would say

The words my ears wanted to hear

In your eyes the were near

Thinking of these, i was on cloud nine

But then i realised your are never mine

I can only imagine those moments

Which usually hurts my sentiments

~ Tanishka Suhane

Ambivalent city

She sprawls carelessly in disdain.

Her beauty hypnotic.

Her chaotic visage

 shuns metaphors.

 She beckons even

 as she repels.

Sweet is her tongue,

sour her mood.

Wild and untamed,

she rises in haste,

 a shabby splendour

still lingering in her gait.

Her ample bosom

 welcomes all.

 Poverty never gets a stigma,

pride never too overbearing..

Of genteel lineage

with her sons bringing

 legendary fame,

 she was the toast of the nation

 once.

Tumultuous is her daily life,

tolerance her creed.

Warm and generous,

 but with resources spent,

her life force propels all

 through adventures

and misadventures,

a living, breathing, dynamic

 symbol of perpetual motion.

She is my metropolis,

crazy and curious.

Where the brightest minds meet

 and go forth to change the world.

Art, literature, film, philosophy

nurtured over centuries.

Where humanity is respected

 and all religions celebrated.

 Where the wealthy

 may not outnumber the poor

 but kindness and morality still

reign.

Decrepit in places,

splendid in others,

a continuous momentum

 of movement,

hope,

effort

and effervescence.

 Order in the frenzy.

 A heart beating fervently

 even in its most somnolent

 moments.

A city of such magnitude

 where millions reside

 in equanimity.

Its gentle folks

nurturing noble values,

 apathetic to caste and creed.

 Pursuing an age-old policy

 of simple living,

high thinking.

 Books are its Bible,

humanity its

pivotal principle.

Effortless yet effective.

Kolkata is a melting pot

 of many religions,

communities,

 cultures.

Eliciting love and loyalty,

passion and poetry

for its kindred character

 of harmonious cohabiting,

joie de vivre,

magnificent festivals,

 mega minds.

The lure of the city

 indescribable,

drawing hundreds into its folds

 Its charm a growing habit

its culture its solace.

Its offspring its pride,

a bounty to the world.

 It's a home that most loathe to

leave behind.

It's a city that's

 refusing to be pushed aside.

-Nandita De nee Chatterjee

<u>*Towards Greater Excellance*</u>

A new day has something to learn

 with a reward to earn.

A new day gives a bag of opportunities

with a tag 'To Never lag'.

 A new day tells to grow strong

and help the weak.

 A new day gives chance

to never leave a hand.

~ Crystal Saldanha

Love memories

Sky is full of stars ,but

 My life is full of tears

Because of you.

 Your my only happiness

 But why you left me alone

 Do you know how much I fell for you

 You were my strongness

Once when you left all of a sudden,

i felt that I was put into a dark room

 Which i can't come out I got angry with my parents

 I couldn't eat,

 i can't smile Even i forgot to smile

 By my behaviour everyone Started to ignore me

 I loosed weight all of a sudden

 I couldn't handle this situation ,

Hands started to shiver, i shouted In room for no reason

My parents though I am facing Serious problems

but i didn't Take much care on myself

 Just the memories killed me

all my soul and body

~ SK Nandhini

Perfect body with a bruised soul

That red-haired girl, Looking out of the window of her castle, Looking Beyond horizons in cold autumn weather , Her soul shiver with cool morning breeze

Do you journey round the universe to seek answers to those unanswerable questions that cloud your heart? That breeze whispered in her ear,

Are you trying to find that healing weed or a healing song ? Do you ask the stars of what could mend your broken soul? That breeze again whispered with cherishing voice ,

She was a broken soul with bruises on every part of her perfect body, A blooming cloud above her head And a flowing river from her burning eyes,

What made u like this? The breeze asked again Unsettled thoughts, caused a ripple effect in your heart Your tongue became too heavy to spits those words Broken wings ripped off your heart, betrayed by love I could feel the heaviness on your shoulder pulling you down and down I could see the emptiness inside of you Turning you into a paper on flames

It's hard to breath, she cried

Then she stood up in the midst her stormy thought And then she gathered all her broken pieces like dead leaves that fell from a tree She hides her soul , with a heavy heart Consealling her bruises within a creamy white perfect body

 She couldn't find an answer like every other day All She wanted was a sliver of hope , To spend the whole day to get mix with the crowd , With dummies all around

She looked into the mirror..., Her lips catch a captivating beautiful fake smile with her eyes sparkling like midnight star Grabbing by her lips and eyes fiercely ,

That ocean of beauty with a raft of confidence, attitude, Well dressed and Posing herself so well, She hides all of her scars beneath a beautiful red dress

No one could see all her bruised soul , All they see is nothing but a perfect body

~ Dr.Saba Tariq

<u>Rooh</u>

Our soul, it never gets old, never gets bold, It's a fragile pure piece of creation which needs love and caring. It's strong in its free state, away from this world but in our body, it's weak, in a constant battle to protect itself from its outer counterpart, our body. Feelings that we feel and talk about, declaring them true and white, sparkling and bright, that feelings that make us happy and light and those which are dark and tight, there are mixed expressions that our soul and body express.

It is said that soul enters our body when we were 3 months old in our mother's womb and from there it grows, and we grow until we are born.

When we are born, our soul is pure and free, but as we grow this world shows its dark forms. Scared, our soul hides within us, hiding it's true state, shifting it's colours like a chameleon, so to look like how the world around it is. It needs a support, it needs a protection and that's why we pray, to keep our soul at peace.

~ Saad Ur Rahman

My Super Hero

He Is my Super Hero,

Sometimes he Became my Villain,

But When its Time For some support

He always behind Me At Every time.

He makes me Strong in Weak situation

And We Call him Dad..

~ Ravikiran

Untold love

Another knight abandons his quest

Nothing changed as he tried to ignore his best

Eyes were watery ,but again blinked as always

His breath was normal, but beats were not

An unfinished lyrics still recites in his brain

A unsung song is still sung by his heart

The weight of the stethoscope seemed heavier to him

Once who carried the guitar on his shoulder

He begged to kiss his dreams for last time

May be they'll smile at him and memories

May be the kiss won't be for the last

But feel the warmth of the embrance you've been searching in

But they forgot that he could fly,

they cut down his wings and made him run

The untold love story mattered to him a lot

As he destroyed himself in the dark light of alcohol and drugs...

-Mallika Dsilva

<u>Oh! My Beloved Moon</u>

Oh! Thou Beloved Moon

When the Universe Embellishes In Darkness,

 in one of those uncountable shimmering Nights,

Come to me

Disencumbering My verses, With those Naked Alphabets,

Cavorting to the shyness of One of those Eplodes,

Scribbled on the parchments.

Oh! Beautiful one

I shalt Mould thou in a poem To efface my love for thee,

Concealing thine ethereal scars Into the crystals of those unsung Syllables.

Oh! Eternal Love

Grace me with those Moonbeams Bleeding & bathing In the Silhouette

of few poems as they endeavour to touch thou.

Oh! Gracious

Ignite the Blue flames of the Oceans, Soothing the rage within,

into those shovel of tears, Lilting along the panacea of words.

Aye! Thou Moon

Thy Euphoria throngs beneath the layers of my skin,

Endowing me with the elixir flavours of life to drink.

But Lo!

Oh! My Beloved Moon

Thine prowess & Sparkles Never Fades.

Oh! Empyrean

I shalt Kiss thy poise with few poems.

~ Mona Dokania

"The Silent Road"

The silent road

Leading souls to their

destinations

Without any distractions

Just with calmness

Not listening to the whispering

and crying

Just going home

Left behind are some sorrows

And some happiness

~ Aditi Hooda

<u>A Pure Beginning</u>

Naked feet on the wet grass;

Rain has just stopped.

I am witnessing a rainbow

Covering my head from above.

I am into the moist bed of hope; at ease.

Not remembering the past.

Not thinking about the constant heavy rain.

Not remembering the dark clouds in my head.

Nothing in mind at all; complete emptiness.

It's a new dawn, a new today

And I am chasing the horizon

In search for some purity;

Some fresh colours of love, pain and gain.

-Ankita Chatterjee

<u>Go Away</u>

Go away Go away... just go away... Otherwise you are gonna be habituated to ME!

Neither you are gonna BE HERE nor I am why to be TOGETHER then ? Go away... just go away...

I'll gonna MISS u.. And You will too at the end why to be CONNECTED then ! Go away... just go away...

We are not gonna MEET again why to stay TOGETHER then? Go away... just go away...

IT'S not in your hand nor mine to be together by the way! then why to make HEARTS fool again? Go away... just go away...

Temporary connections Don't last FOREVER then why to LOVE again? Go away... just go away!!!

~ Aarti Koria

Love

I'm in love with a confused drama

Which makes my mind drown in a beautiful trauma.

That pain which gives me peace,

And makes me dance in a music of harmony.

-Pinky Ray

****

Hey!! My Friend

Hey my friend, don't you worry.

 I'm also getting old with you

There is nothing so special

 Nothing so new

As age is getting caught in brew

 I'm your company

 Soo feel alright

Cheers to our friendship with all my might!

Usha lalwani

<u>*Am I Not Broken?*</u>

That whole night I cried for you like mad!!

I craved for you

I was frustrated

I was broken

By your actions and words.

I decided to leave, and you?

You didn't stop me.

Why?

Were you just finding the ways to throw me away?

Or just pretending to love me?

I didn't know!

I still don't know

I left.

But you, you never come back.

I still love you

I still crave for you

But you, you are busy in your pain!!

Why?

I don't feel pain?

Am I not broken?

Or am I not a human?

I do cry....

I also crave for love daily!

I still feel pain in your Pain,

I left you weeks ago...

But my Heart still standing right over there.

~ Bhawana khetarppal

THE TRUE LOVE

Neither of the friends, nor even my date,

 A three years old pet, was my true mate,

While others were busy, doing their own jobs,

 She was the one, who never made me wait..! . .

Her light brown colour, and the pretty black nose,

She used to bite with fun, and it felt better than a rose,

 I'm again stuck in heartbreaks, and she's no more,

Trying to face the things, let's see how it goes..! .

In the empire of my memories,

she's the lady with the crown,

She was the river, in which I always loved to drown,

Now people say they love me, and ignore me for others,

 They take me for granted, but she never made me feel down..!

Shashwat Trivedi

<u>A poem on hatred feeling of a girl or women in general.</u>

DEPENDENCY tops the list;

Dependent on parents till teenage,

Dependent on husband after marriage,

Dependent on children at old age.

Absence of FREEDOM

No right to make own decisions at home,

Though earn equally to men.

Can't go for work and come back peacefully,

 Fear of being attacked by brutal people

 Real incidents brings fear

 Fear to send children to school

Fear to send children outside to play

Fear to go for night shift

Fear of people

 Fear how to bring up children with good qualities

 Fear for both boy and girl child's growth

 Fear on society as a whole

 Fear on myths

 Myth of praising a newly married girl when good thing happens

 Myth of blaming a newly married girl if bad happens

Thought process of all these makes a woman hate her own life

. People's thinking should change

Way of education should change

Moral life should be led Tradition should not be given up

Culture should be followed

Think and act practically

Teach respect to children

Martial arts should be thought

Self defence knowledge should be there to all

Responsibility should be shared by both wife and husband

In the sense, if a child doesn't behave properly,

People generally blame only mother of the child,

As if the child's father has no responsibility in nurturing the child

All these superstitious beliefs should be changed.

People should walk in the shoes of the other and then speak.

Happiness should be spread all over

Care, sharing should be developed from childhood.

-Mahalakshmi

MICRO FICTIONS

Family Get Together

One day our family of me(nandhini) my brother (suhash) my dad(krishnaswamy) and my brother's friend (dhilip) planned for a trip.as we all know the trip is the best mode for relaxing and enjoyment. If we heard about trip means we will rejoice, the age is not a matter in trip. As all we also we were started rejoicing, the next day fall on Tamil new year we all started the mode on Tamil new year. My brother's friend drove jeep. It was my first trip with my family as it becomes so excited and I started to see and everything from outside the window and pointed each and everything to my dad and bro it seems boring but seeing it for the first time it was really exciting for me. On the 1st we went ranganathittu(birds sanctuary)there we saw many species of birds and there were rare species of birds two eyes was not enough to see all those beautiful birds, and we gone for boating in ranganathittu we saw many crocodiles which was floating near our boat we sawed a crocodile very near and it appears like a stone the boat man went so slowly he showed everything like the birds nests we didn't take many photos. On second, we went for culture. Bulmury was famous for Ganesha temple and lake. There boys were jumping from 6 feet (1.83 m) wall from the lake it were most enjoying moments There we ate fish fry and crab fry as there were chill climate And it was raining and the fish and crab fry was very tasty after eating I was very adamant to put temporary tattoo in hand and finally brother allowed and I inked temporary Scorpio tattoo in my wrist it perfectly suited in my wrist And finally we went to brindhavan garden it was really a lovely place and pleasant atmosphere on entering brindavan garden we went to see aquarium there so many species of fish and some were hiding back of stones and some got afraid while we placed our hands on glass its seems very nice, and we headed to krishnaraja sugar dam it was awesome view from top of the brindavan garden as it was evening the lights in brindha garden makes everyone to feel and everyone in brindhavan garden started to move to somewhere we too joined to see where they are going and here it goes the best moments of life the water dance started water danced perfectly to the tune of song. That was my best moment in life to spend time with dad,brother and with the nature. And finally returned home and talked about this trip and even I share my experiences with friends. The trip may helps spend time with our family .

~ SK Nandhini

Tragedy of life

Somasundaram was a boy who was studying 7th in tirupur. Somasundaram's father(venkat) and mother(krishnaveni) doing small scale business like vessels shop. Somasundaram has 2 sister(thayama, nagamanikam) and 2 brothers(lakshman,chinraj), in that two sister's of Somasundaram where Married They all happily lead their lives. Somasundaram and his brothers were studying. So on one day as usual Somasundaram and Lakshman went to school and another brother(chinraj) was 5 years old, so he was with dad and mother. Venkat and krishnaveni was doing business at that time thayama and her husband(ramakrishnan) came to stay with them 3 to 4 days,after two days Ramakrishnan went out to have alcohol, once it was over he returned home. Ramakrishnan started shouting his wife in bad words at that Krishnaveni came outside to see what's happening between them, while seeing Ramakrishnan scolding her daughter she got angry Ramakrishnan and krishnaveni had fighting in that Ramakrishnan got angry, and he stabbed krishnaveni by seeing this venkat came even Ramakrishnan stabbed venkat as well. They both died before Ramakrishnan tried to escape he got arrested by police. Lakshman joined in hostel for studies and Somasundaram somehow went to Bangalore and stayed in his relative house and finally the last boy named chinraj the neighbors took good care for him so the family got separated. Somasundaram started to work in relative business, they started to treat him like a slave they won't give proper and proper shelter but anyhow he managed till 9years and Somasundaram got married to a girl named sarojini she was very cute but Somasundaram was very doubtful person he started doubting his wife for silly reasons but somehow sarojini managed and gave birth to girl baby named as suguna and one day sarojini went for a movie with neighbor when she returned home Somasundaram got angry and slapped sarojini who fell down and died at that spot. Somasundaram stunned and stared at his wife whether she is acting but all of a sudden he felt coldness in his legs they tried to hide the murder from police. Within three months of sarojini's death Somasundaram got second marriage her name is kaveri. Kaveri was very young girl, Somasundaram was 11 years elder from kaveri but because of kaveri's family situation she got married with Somasundaram she was very kind-hearted girl, kaveri handled every situation gently, and she takes good care of her family. Kaveri and Somasundaram had 2sons (krishna, singaravel) and 2 daughters(geethanjali, bhagyalakshmi) suguna always blame on kaveri for each and everything but kaveri didn't get angry on suguna even kaveri took good care on suguna when compared to kaveri's children Somasundaram watch kaveri whether she is taking care of suguna or not. Somasundaram earned well and stared to save money, and he bought many assets like lands, gold he became much wealthier among his relatives, Somasundaram's assets may calculate in today's budget it will be above twenty crores. Suguna got married, but she didn't adjust with her husband. Geethanjali and krishna got married. Geethanjali gave birth to a son named kailash and krishna had son named naveen so Somasundaram enjoyed a lot with his two grandsons on naveen's second birthday Somasundaram started to behave weirdly and in someday they came to know that Somasundaram has brain tumour. Brain tumour was a he'll sick who can't bear the headache. Somasundaram was shifted to many hospitals for his treatment, doctors suggested doing operation but Somasundaram got sugur. Sugar didn't come to control and doctors lose the hope on operation, Somasundaram got radiation treatment and at that time Somasundaram's family waited outside the room praying the god and hoping that Somasundaram get life, after the treatment doctors gave some hopes so the Somasundaram's family got happy for the betterment but that didn't exist for too long, Somasundaram closed his eyes permanently and Somasundaram sons sold every property and assets and now there are no properties of Somasundaram, but they had the name of Somasundaram's family other than that nothing is there.

SK Nandhini

<u>LIVE INCIDENT..</u>

Sarita's Story

Vanita & Sarita were good friends.

Vanita played with Sarita, her sister Kiran & brother Yash.

They were nice neighbours,

Both used to play together,

Smile & laugh together...

Childhood golden days were well spent together...

On Vanita's Birthday,

Sarita comes & She enjoys in Vanita's Birthday party...

Both were lovely friends...

Years passed,

Both shifted their house,

Still whenever both met

There was pretty a smile on their face...!!

After many years both meet up

Near Vanita's house,

Savita was heading to another house

And was busy in something...

Vanita looks at her,

Sarita gives a big smile to her & waits for the lift to arrive

Vanita don't remember if they had a conversation....

After few days Vanita goes to her

Granny's home in Banglore...

On her Mother's Birthday,

She got news that Sarita is no more..

SHE COMMITTED SUICIDE

Vanita is in great shock..!!!!!

After knowing the reason

Why she committed it,

It was because of the guy who was not ready to marry her...

Sarita was beautiful,

Extremely talented,good in all fields, sports and studies...

Captain of her college...

Everyone loves her even Today....!!!!!

No idea where is Sarita Now...

My Dear,

was he the only person..

ONE LIFE, IS CONNECTED TO MANY

ALWAYS REMEMBER THIS...!!!

-BHAVYA M JAIN S

From Scars to Stars

The society drained her voice. She could feel the devils scratching the walls of her throat. She did speak. No, not her soul, not her heart but just what remained of her body. She was scarred over and over again. The gunshots of the cruel voices suppressed her own. Until she mustered up the courage to break the cage she was trapped in. She glued all her broken pieces together. To show them the treasure she inherited in her. To slap them in their faces with the firm hands of her talent and success. To leave them dumbstruck and flabbergasted. It was her turn to show them what she deserved and what she's worth. It was her time to mute their voices and speak volumes. Oh of course she did it. Only to see their jaw dropping faces. To show them the gems that were embedded in her soul. To elucidate and portray the true definition of passion and determination. It was accompanied with a sense of fulfillment and contentment in her. She achieved the dream the society tried to kill. She sighed with great relief. It felt like heaven to her. She was not a person of words but of actions. She changed their outlook and perspective towards females. Today the world bows down to her and she is the queen!

~ Tamanna Singh

QUOTES

Rahul Gehlot

Have an attitude to win,

but not to defeat others.

****

Making decisions, I always stuck in between "Mind" and "heart".

****

The unbound feelings of mine are still untouched by the people.

****

Fundamentals of life, Express yourself to Impress yourself.

~ Rahul Gehlot

<u>Ashish Goswami</u>

Even her "Black Saree"

Gets faint in front of

"Her Eyes" with "Collyriums

****

My pen has walked more over these papers

As we ever walked together.

****

The day when I fell in love with those beautiful eyes I lost myself

When our lips meet My whole world get flipped

~ Ashish Goswami

Vamshimani

Dear heart, please stop falling

Or else stop beating

****

Yes!! She was a disaster but a beautiful one.

****

His tear was pure because his love was true

****

She is not an angel from heaven, but still, she is the queen
of my heart.

~Vamshimani

Himanshi Tiwari

Don't see the world with someone's lens!! It dosen't fit you, like your own!! Here perception plays the game!!

****

I can be- tipsy without a drink And.. Topsy without a reason..

****

Maybe nights make u feel more alive than the Sunshine's that seem as drawback to our choices, our feels.

****

Not everyone is an artist,

It takes courage to convert your pain into poetry.

~ Himanshi Tiwari

Batul Hashmi

Always say the words of love first to yourself.

****

Its okay when it feels like the whole world is falling apart.
For end is necessary for new beginnings.

****

Walking alone in dark is what make a shooting star
outshine.

****

Shining in the dark is not a big deal for her when she can
even outshine the sun.

-Batul Hashmi

<u>Bhawana khetarppal</u>

I started smiling like a sun, After you came. But now just the broken pieces of moon are left.

****

Ohk! I have a plan (But it didn't work out well) To let my eyes confess What my lips never say.

****

she comes off as strong, But maybe she fell asleep crying, She acts like nothing is wrong, But maybe she's just really good at lying.

****

I still don't know what I will do

I will just smile for no reason looking at you

Your eyes,your cheeks will blow me away

I want you by my side baby,Just stay!!

~ Bhawana khetarppal

<u>Vishwajit RB</u>

I'm responsible

for my every leap.

Equally I'm responsible for my downfall

****

I'm silent,

calm and sensitive too.

Yes!! I am.....

But, that's not my weakness.

Lion hearted doesn't roar everytime.

****

To be a writer is to be a good narrator with imaginative faculty, with skill of ingenuity to club the present scenario with his work of originality.

****

It's good to isolate urself from

this beautifully creepy world.

Just go missing in the quest or

voyage to rediscover ur ability

and find the way back into the

world more stronger.

~ Vishwajit RB

Gritiksha Varma

"We'll share our book shelf..!!" She said to him when she was 18 And here they are, celebrating her 80th birthday together!! They shared their life...!!

****

Cute: When she close her eyes for a kiss and his lips touched her forehead.

****

She was a biology student, He was a maths student.. But their chemistry was amazing.

****

CUTEST PROPOSAL EVER

"You always keep saying 'Hmm',

what's meaning of that?!" She asked

"Hey! Marry me..." he smirked

"Yesss..!!" She giggled

~ Gritiksha Varma

Mohib Ullah

Living with you was not an option...

Living without you was not possible...

Quote: 2

Try look into my eyes...

You will find yourself...

Trapped in my heart...

Quote 3:

The harder you work, the weaker you get and slower you succeed...

The smarter you work, more stronger you get and faster you succees...

Quote 4:

Your Love did a strange magic on me...

I am weaker than i was...

And stronger than i ever could be...

-Mohib Ullah

Co-Authors

G. Vamshimani son, of Mr. Ramesh and Mrs. Renuka, from karimnagar, telangana. Works as product designer and Writing is my passion.
Email:-vamshimani3@gmail.com

Bhawana khetarppal Daughter of Mr. Veer savarkar and Mrs. Kashika. Escaping from pain and her mistakes (according to the world) she call it lessons. She dreams to be a novelist one day. Besides writing, she loves to cook.

I am S K Nandhini and my nick name is tweety, my birthplace is mysore but presently iam staying in Coimbatore (tamilnadu) i just completed my ug degree of B.com in Bharathiyar university.

I *am Ankita Chatterjee. I am from Krishnagar, a small city near Kolkata, West Bengal. I am pursuing my graduation in physics. Writing is one of my hobbies and my instagram ID is my_inside_echoed.*

I'm *Pinky ray, hailing from the cities of nizam and pearls, hyderabad. I'm a student pursuing my bachelors in commerce. Insta handle - @wordsbypinky.*

Tanishka suhane
Class 12th

I'm Tamanna Singh from Faridabad. I'm 15 and I study in Dynasty International School. I love reading books and writing!

Mallika Dsilva a published writer, and loves to write on romance, love and relationships through her poems. Many of her poems are published in different anthologies. She comes from vasai, a small scenic town,in Mumbai and pursuing her Bsc in Mumbai university. Writer's are mysteries, unknown to the world, as they can write and feel things with their wild imagination and passion.So are the readers who join them in their journey and the world needs both of them.

Instagram ID : @silently_writing21

My name is Mohib Ullah. I am from Karachi, Pakistan. I am currently doing A Levels. Insta handle-@mohib54.

My name is Rahul Gehlot, currently Pursuing Master's in Commerce, I started writing a year ago. I'm from Rajasthan but settled in Hyderabad, Telangana.

Myself Ravikiran. I am from Bangaluru. I am completed Diploma. My contact No: 9535975652

I am Batul Hashmi from Indore, India. I am a Dentist by profession. Apart from writing i have skills in art and craft work and painting. You can find me on instagram, I go by the pen name ' mind_echos '

Hey I am Dr.Saba Tariq Rana from Pakistan. I want to treat people medically and with my writings and words too....because mental illness causes more damage than physical one. So I have this mission in my life.

Name- Saad Ur Rahman City- Pune Education- Final Year,Engineering Phone and Whatsapp- 9146643079

Aditi Hooda Rohtak, Haryana BDS-2nd yr 8572072022

My name is Bhaskar Malakar. I stay in a city, named Kailashahar which is situated in the state Tripura of India. I am yet to finish my Engineering degree in civil branch. My contact no. -8730864151

Wordplay my game, stashedviews my pen name, I share my first name with famous insta poet Ms Nikita Gill; a health care professional full-time but poetry runs into me all the time .

I am Shrajan Tiwari, a resident of Kanpur, UP. I am a C.A.final student and passionate about poetry writing, quote creation and blogging. You can reach me at my email id:- tiwaryshrajan786@gmail.com and my contact number 9369526440.

Myself Pratikshya Parhi. From Odisha. She's currently pursuing bsc Zoology hnrs (2ndyr). Writing is her Passion. She's a Cofee free. She craves for each word to give it a meaning. Also the admin of The Soulful Emotions

Mahek Jain was born on 29th day of June,2002. She is studying in class 12 from Assam. She has painting and writing skills. Her hobbies include reading and crafting.

My name's Vishnu E and I'm from Kozhikode, Kerala. I'm 20 years old, founder of the Instagram page @thoughtsndthoughts and I'm currently doing my engineering studies. For contact : vishnuamusafir@gmail.com

Myself Sumit Saha. From Kolkata , Bamangachhi Kulberia

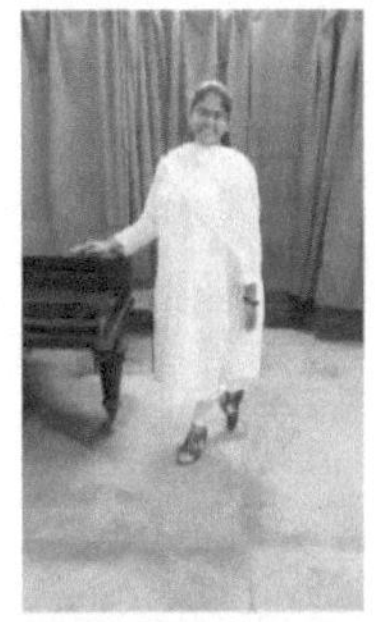

Vidushi Agarwal is a graduate student from, Lucknow Uttar Pradesh. She is also the Vice – President of Creative Society of her college.

I'm Gritiksha Varma from Gujarat I'm 18 and studying BHMS first year Dr. (Future) by occupation, Boxer by aggression, Writer by passion.

Zainab shaikh, Mumbai, BDS (BACHELOR OF DENTAL SURGERY) UPDATE ME AT:- *9920622406 shaikhzainab999@gmail.com*

Myself Himanshi from Jabalpu,r Madhya Pradesh. I'm a student of class 11th

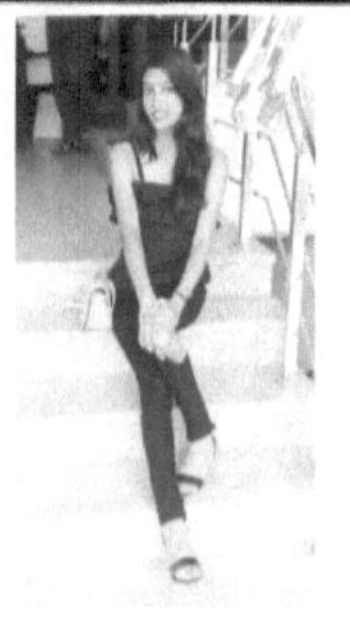

...rti Rohatgi, basically an introvert but ...ve to become an ambivert for ...rvival, and yes an old soul who live in ...r own world, writing is her savior from ...e real world you can check my writings ... Instagram by the name: ...unspokenwor

Niyati Desai I'm 18 and I've developed a kind of interest in writing, expressing my feelings and thoughts through words.

International student from Canada moved from India on 2017 December. Currently living in Vancouver. My email I.D. is Ranvir.rana7473@gmail.com. WhatsApp: +17789576783. Instagram: Ranvir.rn

Crystal Saldanha is a student who is pursuing a Bachelor's degree in Mass Media from Mumbai. She strongly believes that writing gives a person the liberty to express and explore one's thoughts without any boundaries. In her leisure time she reads and writes on her blog.

I'm Kunal Thorat. Bought up in Chakan ,Pune. Currently pursuing B.E. Mechanical engineering. Love to Read novels , exploring the magic of life, and penning them down.

Myself Samreen from Ratnagiri, Maharashtra. Though I studied Science for the last 2 years now am a literature student

Ashish Goswami from patna a boy who loves to write quotes

Myself, Monsumi Borah hailing from Jorhat, Assam. I generally love to ink down my thoughts and currently I am pursuing my PhD under Assam Agricultural University.
Contact
monsumiborao@gmail.com

I am Aarthi Selvam an enigmatic writer in love with words and emotions.I live in the heart of Tamilnadu -Chennai. Get connected with me in
IG:https://www.instagram.com/enigmaticpoetess/?hl=en
Email:aarthiselvam12@gmail.com

Phalguni Jagadeesh, a budding writer with a passion to learn more and improve. A happy soul, finding peace through writing.

Mahalakshmi, from Bangalore. Done with MBA in Finance and Marketing. Was working as an Audit Associate at KPMG, Cochin for few months then transferred to KPMG, Bangalore. Now, a house wife. An amateur writer with a passion to learn more. A singer and loves to do craft work in free time. Energetic learner of new things. Always having the quest to grab knowledge from all fields. Doesn't want to waste free time and utilise it to the optimal level. Wishing to be a bench mark to all.

I'm Mira A Henss and I'm from Chennai, India. I am in my third year of college. You can email me at henssmira@gmail.com or text me at +917395961710.

Shashwat, trying to write down the things whatever he feels, and expecting to live longer in form of words. Currently pursuing Bachelor's of technology and residing in Delhi NCR.

Shipra Khanna from Dehradun has done post graduation in English. Contact number 8920113604

Nandita De is a committed writer, journalist, housewife. Formerly with The Economic Times. Wrote cover stories for The Saturday Statesman and features for Illustrated Weekly of India ,Telegraph, Times of India, Femina, Filmfare, Germany Today Cityscape column, VMM UK, frontierweekly. com.Consulting Editor with Environ.

Name:Usha lalwani City: satna Education :b.com

My name is Tritrishna Ghosh. I have completed my masters in English. I am a teacher by profession. I live in Kolkata, West Bengal.

I'm Bhavya M Jain S,my pen name is Bhavv,I'm from Karnataka, Mysuru.. Writing is my love, My love is my life..!! I write to connect with thy soul & you my dear reader..!!

I am Mona Dokania, Economist and Entrepreneur but by heart.A writer feelings the words make love to poetry.

I *am Aryan Verma, undergraduate at
NIT Hamirpur, from Distt. Pilibhit
Uttar Pradesh
mail:aryanverma19oct@gmail.com
contact:8057233599, 9719051762
instagram_@mysticpen.random*

Ritika Mahto who make every way
possible to Express her feelings through
poetry.And not only poetry travelling
rejuvenates her soul and makes her a
story teller.

Optimistic boy who finds happiness in others smile, lawyer to be, always looking to help and motivate others, who looks at positive outcome of any situation, joyful being who loves to cheer.

Im A 17 And Iam pursuing my diploma in electrical engineering and My wish is that my words should touch many hearts

ABOUT REASONS AND LAUGHTER

Reasons and Laughter is a community which deals with providing services, compiling anthologies, organising competitions and Open Mics, found by Japneet Kaur.

Our main objective is to give a good platform to budding writers to help them grow, even to provide best services and giving wings to their dreams.

Email: ralservicess@gmail.com

Instagram: @reasons_and_laughter

www.ingramcontent.com/pod-product-compliance
Lightning Source LLC
LaVergne TN
LVHW091248180726
843490LV00006B/2228